Praise for *Ben and The Spider Gate*

"A heart-warming and magical tale which will really capture your child's imagination. My son really enjoyed the book and very much identified with Ben and Lox. Each evening he wanted to hear the next instalment and was very captured by the story."

Maria Grachvogel:
London-based Fashion Designer

(Pre-readers)

From Howell's Junior School (Independent Girls' School):

(Year 2 only – July 2015)

The author and ex-Howell's girl Angela Fish visited Year 2 today. Angela's book "Ben and the Spider Gate" isn't out until this September, but we were lucky enough to be sent a sneak preview copy a few weeks ago and so were thrilled to meet the author. We all had masses of questions to ask Angela, not only about the story, but also how she writes her books and where she gets her ideas. We saw illustrations from the book and learned all about the process of how it was published. We then had a real treat when Angela read out an extract from the next book in the series and had a huge surprise when she left us a copy of the new story to read. It won't be out until Spring next year so this is a real thrill – thank you so much, Angela!

St Michael's R C Primary (mixed):

(Years 2, 3 and 4 participated)

Classroom Assistant: I sat in when the class teacher was reading *Ben and the Spider Gate* to the children at story time. It was clear from their faces that they were enjoying it. When it was time to finish the session, even I didn't want the teacher to stop!

Teacher: The pupils were really keen to move on from chapter to chapter. I think they would have been happy to have heard the book all in one go! They were keen to find out more about how the story was written, so Angela Fish was invited in on World Book Day in March and I think she was surprised at the number of questions that they asked. I know that the teachers in the other classes that read the story feel the same way.

Pupils: 'Gran was my favourite – I think she's wise and she's kind.'

'I liked Scoot because he's like my dog – clever but a bit naughty.'

'Ben was naughty to go into the woods and to take Jess with him, but he was only trying to help Lox and the other spiders.'

Extract from a review on 'That's Christmas' (part of 'That's Books' site) by Martin S.
http://thatschristmas.blogspot.co.uk/2015/09/ben-and-spider-gate.html?spref=bl

Ben and the Spider Gate is a fantastic hardback book by Angela Fish. It is a stunningly well-written and delightful book for children and parents and very well-illustrated with some engaging and enchanting artwork throughout the book.

Extract from review by Brian Lee, in *Cowbridge Gem* and also in *Bridgend and Porthcawl Recorder*

Illustrated with some beautiful black and white drawings, it is the kind of book you will enjoy reading to your young children or grandchildren.

Amazon.co.uk review:

My children aged 3 and 6 were hooked by this story and wouldn't let me stop until we finished it all. I liked it as much as they did as it was quite different to the normal children stories we read. We can't wait to read the next one when it's released. ★★★★★

Amazon.co.uk review:

We bought a Kindle Fire for our daughter for Christmas and she really wanted to read this book as the Author came into her school to talk about it. She was really pleased with it! ★★★★

BEN AND THE SPIDER PRINCE

ALSO BY ANGELA FISH

Ben and the Spider Gate

BEN
AND THE
SPIDER PRINCE

Angela Fish

Illustrated by Michael Avery

Book Guild Publishing

First published in Great Britain in 2016 by
The Book Guild Ltd
9 Priory Business Park
Wistow Road, Kibworth
Leicestershire, LE8 0RX
Freephone: 0800 999 2982
www.bookguild.co.uk
Email: info@bookguild.co.uk
Twitter: @bookguild

Typeset in Palatino

Printed and bound in Great Britain by
CPI Group (UK) Ltd, Croydon, CR0 4YY

ISBN 978 1 91087 827 9

British Library Cataloguing in Publication Data.
A catalogue record for this book is available from the British Library.

For my family, with thanks for your encouragement and support.

Contents

1

Lox Asks For Help Again

It was the last day of February and it was snowing. Ben was looking out of his bedroom window at his back garden. He could see the sparrows pecking at the seeds in the bird feeder. It usually made him laugh to see them pushing each other off the feeder, but today he was sad. His gran, who lived with Ben and his mum and dad, was in hospital. She'd fallen on the stairs and had hurt her foot. She'd been in hospital for nine weeks, and Ben really missed her.

He thought about the adventure he'd had last autumn. The magpies had stolen and broken the magic gate to the spider kingdom that was under the hedge at the bottom of Ben's garden. Ben and his best friend, Jess, had helped Lox, the guardian of the kingdom, to find the pieces of the gate. They'd been in trouble for going into the woods on their own, and Ben had hurt himself, but all that seemed like a long time ago now. He was sure that his gran knew a lot more about the strange things that had happened in the garden, and he wanted to talk to her about it.

Ben heard a scratching at his door and when he opened it his little black and white dog, Scoot, rushed in.

'Hello Scoot,' Ben patted the dog's head. 'What are you doing up here?' Scoot wagged his tail hard.

'Good morning sleepyhead,' Ben's mum came into his room as well. 'The hospital have just telephoned and said that Gran can come home tomorrow. Jess's mum said you can wait at their house when Dad and I go to fetch her. All right?'

'That's great!' Ben clapped his hands and Scoot barked.

The next day Ben's dad took him to Jess's house. He was still a bit worried because his mum had told him that Gran would need to rest a lot and that she wouldn't be able to walk properly for a while.

'Don't worry,' Jess's mother said. 'I'm sure your gran will be right as rain very soon.'

Ben looked at Jess. 'What does that mean? *Right as rain*. There's nothing right with rain. It's wet and you can't go out to play.'

'Suppose so,' Jess said, screwing up her nose, 'but if we didn't have any rain then things wouldn't grow. Then we wouldn't have enough to eat and there'd be no water to drink and–'

'All right clever clogs,' Ben interrupted. 'No need to go on about it!'

'Sorry, Ben. Friends?' Jess gave him a "thumbs-up" sign and he did the same.

'I'm sorry too,' he said.

At two o'clock Ben's dad came for him. Ben was so excited! As soon as the car had stopped he jumped out and ran into the house.

'Gran! Gran, where are you?' he called.

'I'm in my favourite chair,' Gran called back.

'I'm glad you're home.' Ben hugged her. 'I want to talk to you about something.'

'Thank you,' Gran patted his back. 'It's good to see you, too. Now, let me get settled and maybe tomorrow we can have a long chat. There are some things I need to tell you too.' She winked at him.

'You mean *secret* things, don't you?' Ben's eyes opened wide.

'Maybe I do, Ben. Maybe I do,' Gran said.

Ben didn't think he'd be able to rest at all that night, but as soon as his mum put out his bedroom light he fell into a deep sleep. Then, just as the light was beginning to creep through his curtains, he thought he could hear someone calling to him. He sat up in bed and looked around. There it was again and it seemed to be coming from somewhere near the window. Ben jumped out of bed and pulled back the curtains. He nearly fell over when he saw who was there. It was Lox! Ben opened the window as quietly as he could and let the spider in.

'Lox! What are you doing here?' Ben bent down and tried to whisper so that his voice wouldn't frighten the spider. 'I didn't know if I'd ever see you again.'

Lox looked up and tried to shout so that Ben would hear him. 'I saw you quite a lot after you found the pieces of the gate, but you didn't see me. I was afraid because there were so many people around so I stayed hidden. This isn't really the right time for me to be out now, it's so cold, but I need your help again, Ben.'

'Oh, Lox. What's the matter?' Ben frowned. He wasn't sure if he really wanted another adventure. He'd been quite scared last year when he and Jess had been lost in the woods.

'The Spider Queen and the Spider Wizard were very grateful to you for helping us with the gate,' Lox said, 'but we have a much more serious problem now, and I've been sent to talk to you.' He shivered and Ben could see how tired he was.

'What is it? You know I'll help if I can.' Ben started shivering as well.

'It's the Spider Prince.' Lox ran up and down the window sill. 'He's very ill. The wizard has tried everything but nothing's worked. There's one last magic potion to try, but the ingredients are hard to find. They work much faster if they're fresh, but dried ones are all right too. The wizard had some dried ones in his store room but they've been stolen and–'

'Stolen?' Ben shouted out loud. Lox covered his ears with his front legs. 'What do you mean? Who would do that? It couldn't have been the birds again. They're too big to go into your cave.'

Lox shook his head. 'No, it wasn't the birds. We think it was Queen Aranya's sister. She's always wanted to be queen, and she's always causing trouble.'

'Do you ever have a Spider King, Lox?' Ben asked.

'Yes,' Lox said. 'There are six queens in a row, but then the seventh leader will be a king. Each queen chooses who will be the next one in charge. It doesn't have to be the eldest of her children though. She has to choose the one who she thinks will be the best leader. Spindra was the eldest daughter of the old queen, and that's why she's so jealous of her sister.'

Ben chewed on his bottom lip. 'So she wouldn't be very happy if I helped you. Do you think she would try to hurt me?'

'She wouldn't be able to when you're the size

you are now,' Lox said. 'We'd have to be careful if you became small again, like when you helped us with the gate, but there are many others who would watch out for you. The wizard's magic can be very powerful but he really needs the fresh ingredients for the potion now. Do you think you can help us?'

Ben scratched his head. 'I don't know, Lox. What would you want me to do? I can't go outside the garden on my own again. I promised my mum and dad. How quickly do you need to find these things? What are they?'

Lox stood up on his four back legs and waved the others around in front of him. 'We think it's best if you come into the kingdom and talk to the wizard. If you can't help, he'll understand.'

Ben shook his head slowly. 'But how can I meet with the wizard? I can't get into the cave when I'm this size, and I don't know what happened to make me small the first time we met.'

Lox looked up. 'Ask your gran, Ben. Ask your gran. Now, I have to get back. The wizard says he can't cure the prince but he can keep him alive for a little bit longer. I'll come back in three days' time.'

Ben opened the window and Lox ran out and down the side of the house.

2

Gran Tells Ben The Secret

The next day was very windy, and after breakfast Dad said he was going to do some gardening. Mum was going to the shops and, once she'd gone, Ben and his gran sat down on the settee.

'Now then,' Gran said, 'what's this important thing you want to talk about?'

Ben wriggled in his seat. 'Do you remember the story that I told you last year about the spider gate and the magpies?' Gran nodded. 'Well, it wasn't a story. It really happened. I don't know how I became small. I just fell asleep in the garden and when I woke up I was little! You do believe me, don't you?'

Gran patted his hand. 'Of course I do. I knew all along.'

Ben's mouth fell open. 'How did you know? Why didn't you say anything?'

'Slow down,' Gran laughed out loud. 'I have a lot to tell you, but you must promise to keep it a secret. I don't think many people would understand, or even believe you if you told them, but when I was eight – a little bit older than you – my father took me out into the garden one day and said that he had something important to tell me. He said it was a secret that had been in the family for a very long time, but that only one person at a time could use it.'

'What do you mean by *use* it?' Ben interrupted.

'I'm coming to that,' Gran said. 'My father told me that his father had passed the secret to him, but it didn't mean that it always had to be done like that. You know, from parent to child. It could be anyone – family or friend – but, once it had been passed on, you couldn't have it back. The secret was the way to become small, and also how to return to normal size again.'

Ben bounced up and down on the settee. 'Where did the secret come from in the first place?'

'Don't rush me,' Gran said, 'or I might forget something important. Well, my father didn't know where the secret came from. He'd been told that many years ago there was a wise woman who lived in a cave in the mountain, on the far side of the valley. Someone in my family helped her and their reward was a rhyme that could be used to shrink the person who used it, and another to bring them back again.'

'Do you know the rhyme? Is that what the secret is? Can you tell me?' Ben's cheeks were getting redder and redder.

'Yes, Ben, I do know the rhyme and I will tell you soon, but there are some other things you need to know first. It's important that you listen carefully. You must tell me if you don't understand what I'm saying. You will, won't you?' Gran looked at Ben and he nodded quickly. 'Well, each person who is given the secret can only use it seven times in their life. It doesn't matter when it's used – it could be all in one year, or spread out over many years. The thing to remember is that once each rhyme has been used seven times it has to be passed on to someone else.'

Ben frowned. 'If you have the secret right now, then how did I become small last year? Why have you kept it for so long? Didn't you want to give it to Mum?'

Gran smiled at him. 'Full of questions, aren't you, lad? I didn't give it to your mum because it just didn't feel right. She wasn't really interested in the birds and the insects and the trees – all the things that I loved. That's mostly how I used the rhyme, so that I could find out more about them. Sometimes I was able to help them, like you did with Lox, but I'll tell you about all that another time. I used the rhymes five times in the first two years, but I decided to keep the last two for a while longer. After I went to the Grammar School I was so busy with homework and new friends that I never really thought much about the secret. When I was older I married your grandfather, and a few years later your mum was born, so I had even less time to think about it. I used it once more just after you were born.'

'But what about me?' Ben asked. 'How did it happen to me?'

Gran paused for a moment. 'There's another thing you need to know. Whoever has the rhyme can make someone else small too, but if they *tell* anyone else what the rhyme is, they lose the power. It also counts as one of the seven times. Last year you seemed as though you were a little bit lonely. I know it's not easy living so far away from most of your friends, so I thought I'd give you an adventure.'

'But why had you kept the last chance for so long?' Ben moved to the edge of his seat. 'Does that mean that you can't use the rhyme anymore? Doesn't that make you sad?'

Gran smiled. 'I kept it because I thought I might like to have one more adventure, but when I saw you asleep on the grass I just knew it was right to give it to you instead. Besides, I think I'm getting too old for such things. The rhyme makes you small but it doesn't make you young!'

'So how old are you, Gran?' Ben asked.

'As old as my tongue and older than my teeth, young man,' she laughed. 'Now, stop interrupting. There's a lot more to tell you but you might want to fetch your notebook and pencil.'

Ben rushed up the stairs to his room. He found his notebook and pencil, and he ran back down again.

'Ready. What's next?' he said.

3

Ben Learns The Magic Rhymes

Gran told Ben to write down what she told him. There were the two rhymes and the way that the secret could be passed on. He turned to a clean page in his notebook and waited.

'Right, the first rhyme is the one to make you small,' said Gran. 'It's better if you try to remember it, but be very careful about saying it out loud and doing the actions at the same time, as you could end up using all your chances in one day! It might be better if I just teach you both the rhymes before I pass over the secret to you. What do you think?'

Ben scratched his head. 'Yes. That means I'll have more time to make sure I know the rhymes properly. Is it a lot to learn?'

'Not really,' Gran smiled at him, 'but you have to make sure you get it right, especially when you want to come back. Now, write this down. I'll say it slowly.'

Ben took his pencil and wrote down exactly what his gran said.

Hold my breath and count to four,
breathe out slow and count four more.
Turn three circles, count to ten,
touch the floor, turn once again.
Close my eyes and touch my nose,
now make me small from head to toes!

Ben opened his eyes wide and his mouth too! He wanted to try out the magic rhyme so much, but he knew he'd have to wait until Gran was ready to pass over the secret. She began to recite the rhyme for getting back to normal size. It was exactly the same, except for the last line which was "now make me *big* from head to toes!"

Ben stopped writing. 'What happens if I say them the wrong way around? Will I become a giant? Or even smaller if I'm already small?'

'No,' Gran shrugged her shoulders. 'It doesn't seem to work like that. I don't know why, but as long as you say the words in the right order and do the actions properly then the magic happens. You understand that it's important to learn the words exactly, don't you? Just imagine how scared you'd be if you were small and couldn't remember how to become your proper size again.'

Ben shivered. 'Ooh, yes, but what if I was in a small place and said the rhyme, but there wasn't enough room for me to be big in there?'

Gran took off her glasses and rubbed her eyes. 'Well, that would be a bit silly, wouldn't it? You'd have to make sure you were in a good place first. Now, just one more thing and then I think I need to rest. You remember that I said you could use the rhyme for someone else to become small? Well, it's very easy. Instead of saying 'me' in the rhyme, you just put their name instead, but *you* have to do the actions. You must be careful if you do this, and you shouldn't really do it unless the person agrees. I know I didn't ask you when I did it, but I guessed you'd be excited about the adventure. If you do decide to use the magic like this, you need to think carefully about how you'll bring the person back again. You wouldn't want to lose someone, would you?'

Ben thought for a moment. 'I suppose it would have to be for something important, wouldn't it? I mean, to use the magic on someone else?'

'Yes,' Gran agreed, 'and it would have to be someone you trusted very much, because you'd have to tell them something about the secret wouldn't you? Anyway, that's a lot for you to think about for now. Go and help your dad in the garden for a while and try not to think about the secret too much. I expect you'll have lots more questions for me tomorrow.'

Ben went into the kitchen and pulled on his coat and his boots. His head was bursting with all the things his gran had told him. He just couldn't wait for tomorrow!

The next afternoon, when Ben arrived home from school, he ran upstairs and slammed his bedroom door. Mrs Jenkins, who lived at the end of the lane and had called in to see Gran, jumped and spilled her tea. She mopped it up with a tissue, and said she'd leave now that Ben was home.

'Oh dear,' Gran said, 'it sounds like Ben's had a bad day. Would you mind calling him for me on your way out? I still can't manage the stairs properly.'

Mrs Jenkins shouted up to Ben and then left. After about ten minutes he came down the stairs very slowly. He went into the kitchen to fetch a glass of milk, and then took it into the living room.

'Hello, Ben.' Gran patted the seat next to her. 'Come and sit here and tell me what the problem is. Bad day at school?'

He sniffed. 'Sort of.'

'What kind of answer is that? Come on, you can tell your Gran, can't you? Then we can talk some more about the secret.'

Ben sat down. 'Well, you remember I told you about the new girl who came to our school at the start of this term? Miss James put her on the table with Jess and me, and said we should look after her. She didn't know anyone else.'

15

'Yes,' Gran said, 'I remember. Her name's Kelly or something like that? So what's happened? I thought you were all getting along well.'

Ben sighed. 'We were, but ever since the half-term holiday they don't want to play with me, or even talk to me much. They just keep giggling together. I tried to ask Jess if I'd done something wrong but she didn't really answer me. She just said "no" and ran off.'

Gran rubbed the end of her nose. 'You know, sometimes friendships change, or even end, as you grow older. You have other friends in your class, don't you? Maybe you should spend a bit more time with them?'

'But Gran,' Ben said, 'Jess has always been my best friend and I've been hers. We like the same things and the same games and everything.'

Gran could see that he was upset, so she thought it was best to talk about something else until he calmed down. She told him to fetch his notebook again and to read her the rhymes. He managed quite well, but there were a few words that Gran had to help him with. Then he tried it with the actions, and they both laughed when he fell over.

'Now then. Any questions about anything I've told you so far?' Gran asked.

Ben linked his hands behind his neck and rocked in his seat. 'Yes. If I used the rhyme and I went off exploring or something, wouldn't Mum and Dad wonder where I was? I'd be in trouble if they

thought I'd gone out on my own again, wouldn't I?'

'There's something else you need to know about the secret,' Gran said. 'When you use the rhyme, it's as if time doesn't move at all. It doesn't matter how long you're away, when you come back it's the same time as when you left. Didn't you notice that last year?'

'Not really,' Ben replied. 'I wasn't small for very long – I just met Lox and we found the first piece of the gate. If it was you that made me small, how did you know when to make me big again?'

'I was watching you all the time,' Gran frowned. 'I was a bit worried that Scoot would think you were something to play with, but he was sleeping in the shade. You have to be very careful when you're small. There are lots of things that could hurt you. You'd make a nice meal for the magpies!' Gran poked him in the stomach, and they both started laughing again.

Ben went upstairs to put his notebook away and to think about what his gran had told him. Lox would be coming back on Wednesday. Ben knew the secret now, but he didn't know if his gran would let him use it just yet. He wanted to talk to Jess about it but he didn't think she'd listen. The other problem was that he didn't want to share the secret with Kelly.

4

Ben Tells Gran About The Spider Prince

Ben woke early on Wednesday morning, and climbed out of bed as quietly as he could. He opened the curtains and looked out for Lox. There was no sign of the spider, so Ben put on his dressing gown and started drawing a picture of the two magpies that had broken the spider gate, as well as one of Lox. He had just started drawing Scoot when he heard a tap on the window. Lox was waving at him, so he opened the window and the spider climbed in.

'Hello Lox,' Ben said, 'are you all right?'

'Hello, Ben,' Lox shook a big raindrop from his back, 'just a bit wet. Did you talk to your gran?' Ben nodded. 'Did she tell you what you needed to know?'

Ben sighed. 'Gran told me about the secret but she hasn't passed on the power, so I can't use it yet. I can ask her if she will, and then I can help you. I'll do that today when I come home. I promise.'

'I'll tell the queen and the wizard. When's the next time that you don't have to go to school?'

'That's Saturday,' Ben said. He counted on his fingers. 'Today is Wednesday, then Thursday, Friday, Saturday.'

'Can you meet me near the spider gate on Saturday morning?' Lox asked. 'If you have the secret then I'll take you into the kingdom. If you can't come, or you don't have the secret, hang a piece of ribbon out of your window and I'll come to see you as soon as I can. Thank you, Ben.'

Ben opened the window and Lox ran out. Ben watched until the spider was out of sight, then he began to get ready for school.

By Friday Ben had still not spoken to his gran about the secret. Every time he tried to, something happened to stop them talking. There were visitors on Wednesday, and then Gran had to go back to the hospital on Thursday for a check-up, and was late coming home. Ben was sad that he might not be able to help Lox after all. He decided that as soon as he was home from school he'd ask Gran if she would pass on the secret to him. He'd have to tell her about Lox, but he was sure she'd understand. He'd been practising the rhymes and he thought he knew them now.

When he opened the kitchen door at four o'clock he knew that Gran was on her own. She was sitting at the kitchen table reading the newspaper.

'Hello,' she smiled at him. 'Home already? Would you like some milk or some juice?'

'Hi, Gran,' Ben said. 'Milk, please. Can we talk some more about the secret? I need to ask you something.'

'Of course we can,' she said. 'Let's sit here at the table. Your mum and dad won't be home from work for a while, so we have plenty of time. Now, what's worrying you?'

'It's about the secret.' Ben wriggled in his chair. 'Lox needs my help again, and if I can't go into the spider kingdom to meet the wizard and the queen, the Spider Prince might die. I need to be small again, but you said that once the rhymes had been used seven times each they wouldn't work unless the secret was passed on, didn't you?' Gran nodded. 'So that means you can't make me small, I have to have the secret myself.'

'I don't know, Ben. I'll have to think about it.' Gran frowned. She wanted to help him but she was afraid that he wasn't really old enough to take care of the secret, and use it safely.

'Lox wants me to meet him tomorrow,' Ben said. 'There's not a lot of time left, Gran. I promise I won't use the magic unless I have to, and I won't tell anyone else about it. Jess knows about what happened last year but she doesn't know about the secret. I don't think she'd want to anyway.'

'Things are still not right, then?' Gran asked. Ben shook his head. 'Never mind. Give me a little while to think. I promise I'll tell you my answer before you go to sleep tonight.'

Later that evening Ben went to say goodnight to his gran. She told him that she would hand over the secret to him in the morning. Ben was so excited that it took him a long time to go to sleep. He dreamed all night long about dark caves, spiders with pointed hats, and a big bottle of yellow liquid.

5

Gran Gives Ben The Power

The next morning, after breakfast, Ben and Gran sat at the kitchen table. She looked a little bit worried and he was afraid that she might change her mind.

'Ready, Ben? This might seem a little bit strange, but you need to listen carefully and do what I tell you without saying anything at all. If you interrupt me while I'm handing over the power to use the magic then it won't work. I'll write down the words and the actions for you, but I'll keep them somewhere safe until you're older. You have to be very sure about the person that you give the power to.'

Ben leaned across the table. 'Yes, Gran, but I couldn't give the power away until I'd used it all, could I?'

'Well, that's the thing,' she said. 'You could if you wanted to, but it would mean that you couldn't use the magic again. The person you passed it on to would start with their seven straightaway.'

Ben pulled down the corners of his mouth. 'Is

23

that why you don't want me to know this part then? In case I give it away too soon?'

'That's right,' she told him, 'but don't worry about that now. We need to do this before your mum and dad finish the shopping if you want to go and see Lox this morning.'

She took Ben's notebook and wrote in it for a few minutes. Then she tore out the page and put it in her pocket. She asked him to fetch the vinegar bottle, the salt shaker, the pepper pot, and a bowl of water. He put them on the table and then sat down again. Gran asked him to hold out his hands, and she put three shakes of salt on one hand and three shakes of pepper on the other. Then she put the vinegar bottle in front of her.

'Ready, Ben?' she asked. 'Now remember, not a word until I tell you to speak. Only make the movements I tell you. It won't take long.'

He was a little bit afraid, but excited as well. He watched as his gran held her hands just over his. She began to whisper. Then she picked up the vinegar bottle and tipped three drops onto Ben's right hand, and three onto his left hand. With the middle finger of her left hand, she mixed the pepper and the vinegar. With the middle finger of her right hand, she mixed the salt and the vinegar. Then she took both of Ben's hands and put them together.

'Keep them tight. Don't let the vinegar run away. No! Don't say anything,' Gran warned him, just as he was about to ask why.

She took a feather from her pocket and Ben gasped. It was so pretty, and he'd never seen one like it before. It was shiny green and blue, and had some gold shapes on it. It was long and wispy at the ends, and Gran began to wave it over his head then down his arms. She told him to put his hands out, and she brushed the feather over them. He shivered.

Gran put the feather on the table and took a small stone from her pocket. It looked like glass, but it was cloudy and it had a hole in the middle. She put the bowl of water in front of Ben and dropped the stone into it. His eyes opened wide as he watched the stone. It plopped into the water and sank to the bottom, but then began to float around the bowl as if it was made of cork. He had to bite on his lip to stop himself from speaking! Gran lifted the bowl.

'Take three small sips,' she told him, 'but don't swallow the stone.'

He sipped the water. It didn't taste nasty, but it wasn't the same as usual. Gran put the bowl on the table and stood behind Ben. She put her hands on his shoulders and tapped three times. She did some more whispering and then stood in front of him. She didn't say anything for a minute, and then she put her hands over his eyes.

She said out loud, 'Now the power is yours. Use it wisely.'

Ben felt a bit dizzy and Gran told him to wait a few minutes before talking. She took the stone from the bowl and dried it, and told him that it was called an adder stone. It had magical powers, and could protect its keeper against evil spells. She threaded a piece of string through the hole, tied a knot in it and put it around Ben's neck. She told him to look through the hole if he ever felt that he might be in danger. She said that it had come from the wise woman on the hill. She'd found it on the shore of the magic lake, high in the mountains. Then Gran told him to go upstairs and pack his rucksack for his journey into the spider kingdom.

'What do you think I should take?' Ben asked. 'I'm only going to meet the wizard so that he can tell me what I need to do.'

'I know,' Gran said. 'You'd better take your torch and I think you ought to take Scoot's whistle as well. Just in case you get into any trouble. If he starts barking near the hedge I'll know something's wrong.' When Ben and Jess had been lost in the woods Scoot had found them when he heard them blowing the whistle.

Ben went to his room and found his rucksack. He packed his notebook and pencil and the things his gran had suggested. When he was back in the kitchen Gran handed him a ball of yellow wool. He looked puzzled.

'What's this for?' he asked. 'I don't think the spiders want me to knit for them!'

'Silly boy,' she said. 'Do you remember the film we watched about the Greek prince who had to go into a big maze where there was a monster? How did the prince find his way out?'

Ben thought for a moment. 'I know! A lady had given him some magic string, and he tied it to a tree before he went into the maze. When he wanted to come out he wound it up until he was back at the beginning.'

'Well done,' Gran said. 'So, use this wool in the same way.'

Ben thought this was a bit silly, because he knew that Lox would be with him all the time, but he promised his gran that he'd do as she said. He put on his coat and boots, and went down to the bottom of the garden.

6

Ben Meets The Spider Wizard

Ben couldn't see Lox at first and he wasn't sure if he should say the rhyme. If he said it and then Lox didn't come, he'd have wasted a turn. He leaned against one of the big trees. Suddenly he felt something tickling his ear. Lox was hanging from a cobweb just above him!

'Ready Ben?' Lox asked. 'Come on, do what you need to do and then we can go.'

Ben took a deep breath, then said the rhyme and did the actions. He had the same dizzy feeling that he'd had before, and he sat down quickly. After a moment he felt fine. He stood up and realised that the grass was now taller than him. He'd done it. He'd made the rhyme work!

Lox and Ben went under the hedge towards the spider gate, but before they went in Ben tied the end of the yellow wool around a low branch. Lox looked at him a bit strangely, but he didn't say anything until the guards had let them through the gate.

'Stay close to me,' he said. 'You'll find our world very different from yours, but I'll keep you safe.'

Ben could hardly see in the cave, so he took out his torch. Lox told him to keep his hand over the beam so that he didn't frighten the other spiders. Ben followed Lox through a long tunnel that he guessed was under the lane at the back of his garden. Then they went down a slope. In front of them were seven openings, and Lox scuttled through the middle one. Ben followed, remembering to unwind the wool as he went.

He was becoming used to the dim light and he could just about see some shapes in the side passages. He could hear a lot of rustling noises and it made him feel a little bit afraid, so he hurried to keep up with Lox. After a while the spider stopped.

'This is the wizard's room,' Lox said. 'I'll go and fetch him and he can explain everything to you. The queen will be listening, but she'll only meet with you if you can find the ingredients. Wait here!'

He ran through a hole at the back of the room. Ben looked around and shivered. He'd been all right when Lox was there, but he didn't feel so brave now. It felt as though there were lots of eyes watching him, but he couldn't see anyone at all. He felt a light touch on his sleeve and he jumped.

'Sorry. I didn't mean to frighten you. Are you Ben?' A big spider was right next to him. 'I've heard so much about you, and how you helped with the spider gate. I hoped I could meet you in person. I'm Spindra. The queen's sister.'

Ben jumped back. He really was afraid now. This was the spider who was supposed to have stolen the wizard's ingredients. She moved closer to him and began to pull gently at the yellow wool.

'Pretty,' she said. 'It would be good for spinning. It's so tiring having to make all my own.'

She pulled a little harder and started to wind the wool around two of her legs. Ben knew that she must have untied it, or bitten through it at the spider gate. He tried to tug the wool away but she hissed at him, so he dropped the ball and ran. He didn't know where he was going, but he wanted to get away from Spindra as quickly as he could.

He went up one passageway but it was a dead-end. He went back and tried again. Another dead-end. He could hear something behind him, and he was just about to run again when he tripped over a tree root. He felt the adder stone dig into him as he fell, so he took it out and held it in front of one eye.

Through the hole in the stone he could see that there was a bright yellow cobweb all across the opening of the passageway in front of him. If he'd run into it he would have been trapped. When he took the stone away from his eye, he couldn't see the web. Gran had been right – the stone was magic! He shone his torch at the web and he could see Spindra watching him. Ben waved the torch at

her and she ran away. When he stood up, Lox was behind him.

'Come on,' the spider said. 'It's all right now. Just follow me. The wizard's waiting.'

They ran back to the wizard's room. Ben was amazed at the colours all over the spider's back. There was a silver star, a gold moon and lots of red and green spots. The wizard was bigger than Lox but he wasn't scary at all. He told Ben to sit down on the floor.

'Thank you for coming,' he said. 'I know this must be very strange for you, but I can only go outside at night, and we knew that you wouldn't be able to meet me then. Lox has explained the problem to you?' Ben nodded. 'Good. Then this is what I need.'

He began to list the things he wanted for the magic potion, but Ben couldn't keep up.

'Wait,' Ben said. 'Please can you talk more slowly? Can I write these things down so that I can remember them?'

The wizard agreed and began again. 'I need seven petals from the Fairy Wing Flower, seven leaves from the Dragon's Breath Fern, and seven tears from a true friend. You can see what the plants look like in my potions book here, and how to keep them fresh when you've collected them. You can catch the tears in this tube.' He passed it to Ben. 'You must collect them all in the same week. The prince is very ill and I can't keep him alive for much longer.'

'How much time do I have?' Ben asked.

'Tonight there will be a full moon,' the wizard said. 'You have until the next full moon. After that it will be too late. Lox will take you back and answer any more questions for you. Goodbye Ben, and good luck.'

When they were back at the gate and the guards had let them through, Ben asked Lox if he knew how much time there was between the full moons. Lox wasn't sure and told Ben to ask his gran. He waited until Ben had said the rhyme and was big again and steady on his feet. Then he said he'd come to see Ben on the following Saturday.

7

Ben And Gran Begin The Search

In the kitchen, later that day, Ben dragged a chair across to the wall where the calendar was hanging. Last year, when he'd wanted to know about the autumn, Gran had shown him how to mark off the days. It was March now and there were thirteen crosses on the page. Ben could see that there was a small picture of a moon in the box for Saturday – that was today. Did it mean that the calendar showed when every full moon would be? Ben looked at the page for April and he could see the same moon picture in the box for Sunday the twelfth of April. Just then Gran came into the kitchen.

'Hello,' she said. 'Trying to work out when the holidays start?'

'No,' Ben answered. 'I want to know how long it is between tomorrow and this day.' He pointed to the April page on the calendar, 'and I want to know if this picture means it will be a full moon on those days.'

Gran frowned. 'Yes it does, but what are you up

to, young man? I hope you're not planning to do anything that you shouldn't?'

'Not really.' He grinned at her. 'I've promised to help Lox and the wizard find some things and it has to be done before the next full moon. Can you help me?'

Ben explained that he'd been asked to find some unusual plants, but that he'd forgotten to ask the wizard or Lox where to look for them.

'That was a bit silly,' Gran said. 'They could be anywhere.'

'I know,' he said, 'but I was a bit scared when I was in the spider caves. Oh–' he tapped himself on the head, 'I forgot – there might be something in my notebook.' He opened it at the pages where he'd drawn the pictures of the plants.

'See,' he pointed. 'This one's called the Fairy Wing Flower, and this one's the Dragon's Breath Fern. It says that the flower sometimes grows under a tree, and the fern grows near a stream.'

'Well that's not much help,' Gran said. 'The stream could be anywhere, and there are hundreds of trees around here. What type of tree?'

Ben looked puzzled. 'I don't know. There was a picture of a tree but I didn't have time to copy it properly. It had funny-shaped leaves, and it was a bit like those trees in the park next to Mrs Jenkins's house. You know, the ones where the birds were fighting over the berries last year.'

'I think you mean the rowan trees,' Gran said. 'So, as long as the wizard didn't mean one particular tree, that could be a good place to look.'

Ben wanted to rush off right away but his gran reminded him that he'd said the ingredients had to be found in the same week. If he found the flower quickly and then couldn't find the fern until another week, he'd have to go back for more flowers. If they really were magic then Gran didn't think it was a good idea to take too many.

'Now, what about the fern?' she asked him. 'Any thoughts on that?'

Ben shook his head. 'Nothing. What can I do? Can we look on the computer for ideas?'

Gran nodded. 'I suppose so, but I won't be much help to you. I'm not very quick with it you know, but I can help with spelling, and reading what you find. We could have a look in your dad's gardening books as well, but I don't think these kinds of plants would be in there. What about the library?'

Ben groaned. 'Oh Gran! That'll take ages. It's much quicker on the computer.'

'I'll make a deal with you then,' she said. 'I'll help you with the computer once or twice in the week, but then you come to the library with me on Saturdays. Not everything's on the computer, you know.'

'All right,' he agreed, 'but I have to find out where to look as soon as I can. Is it a long time until the holidays?'

Gran looked at a piece of paper that was pinned up near the calendar. Ben's mum had put it there to remind her of all the school events.

'Look,' Gran pointed. 'You break up in two weeks and a few days. Then you have another twelve days before the next full moon.'

They agreed that they'd begin looking for clues about the Dragon's Breath Fern the next day. Ben knew that Gran still couldn't walk too far, so he hoped that the ferns were nearby. There was no way that he could go out on his own, and even if Jess was still talking to him properly, he knew she wouldn't go with him. He had an idea about the last item on his list – the seven tears – but he didn't want to tell Gran just yet.

The next two weeks seemed to go by so slowly for Ben. He went to school and tried hard to make up with Jess, but she still preferred to spend time with Kelly. Twice a week Gran helped him to search on the computer for clues about the plants, but they found nothing.

On two Saturdays Ben's mum drove him and Gran to the library in the nearby town. Gran knew the lady who worked there and she explained that Ben was looking for a book on unusual plants for a project that he was doing. He smiled when she said that, but it was true in a way, wasn't it? They stayed for two hours each time but they still didn't find anything.

8

The Book

On the last day of term Ben was surprised to see Gran waiting for him at the school gates. She told him that the lady from the library had telephoned her. She'd found a very old book in the storeroom, and she thought that it might be just what Ben was looking for. They hurried into the library, and the lady said that Gran could take the book out on her library card. Ben was so excited that he hopped all the way to the bus stop.

'Do you think this is the right book for us?' he asked. 'It's really old, isn't it? Can we look at it right away?'

Gran laughed out loud. 'I think I deserve a cup of tea first, don't you?'

When they were home, Ben sat at the table with Gran and opened the book. He turned the pages carefully because they were quite stiff. There were lots of pictures, but Ben found it hard to read some of the words because they were handwritten. Gran, though, seemed to be able to read them easily.

She said that the book was full of stories from a very long time ago, and some of them said things about special plants. People believed that these plants had magic powers. Ben wriggled on his seat. He hoped that Gran could find something about the fern, but after half an hour she hadn't found anything.

'That's enough for now,' she said. 'I might have a look this evening, but otherwise we'll start again tomorrow.'

Ben woke up early the next morning but then he remembered that he didn't have to go to school and that he could look at the story book again. He felt a little bit sad that Jess wouldn't be coming over to his house. He'd asked her but she said that she was going to stay at Kelly's house for the first week of the holidays. He went downstairs and into the living room. It was very quiet, as his mum and dad had already gone into town for the day.

Ben found the story book on Gran's chair, and as he picked it up he could see a piece of paper sticking out of it. He opened the book at that page and he nearly dropped it on the floor! There in front of him was a picture of the Fairy Wing Flower. It was growing in a circle underneath a big rowan tree. Gran had been right. He couldn't understand what the writing said, so he put the piece of paper back and went to find his gran.

'You found it – the flower!' he shouted. 'But I can't read what it says.'

'Yes,' she said. 'They don't grow under every rowan tree so we have to hope that we're lucky with the ones in the park. I'm going to keep reading to see if there's anything about the fern. That's the one we really need help with. Why don't you get your bird book out and do some drawings while I read, or you could take Scoot out into the garden?'

Ben called to Scoot. The little dog wagged his tail hard and followed him. They played ball for half an hour, and then he did some more training with Scoot's special whistle. He looked up and saw that Gran was waving to him from the kitchen doorway, so he began to run. She must have found something!

Gran showed Ben the book again. She had found a story about some little people who lived in the woods, and how a kingfisher had helped them to chase off a water rat who was stealing their food. On the second page was a picture of the plants that the little people grew, and one of them was the Dragon's Breath Fern.

'What does it say?' Ben asked Gran. 'Does it say where it grows?'

'It says that the fern was made from the breath of green dragons. The little people let the dragons live

44

under the roots of the trees, and the dragons helped the little people by making the fern for them to eat.'

'Wouldn't the dragons have burned the plants?' Ben asked. 'The ones in my computer game and in my story book all breathe out fire.'

'Well,' Gran read from the book, 'these were tiny dragons, and their breath was cold like frost, so the plant was silvery, and looked like snowflakes. People believe it can still be found near the part of a stream where the kingfishers dive.'

Ben opened his bird book and found a picture of a kingfisher. It had bright blue and orange feathers, and a pointed beak. He remembered seeing one when his dad had taken him out with Scoot once. They'd crossed the park and walked around the edge of the woods until they came to the stream. The path followed the stream back into the woods and that's where they'd seen the bird, which was hunting fish, and it had flown quickly and low over the water.

'Oh yes!' he said. 'I've seen one on the other side of the woods. Do you think it might still be there?'

Gran thought for a moment then said that it was quite likely, but she wouldn't be able to take Ben there. Her foot was a lot better but the path in the woods was bumpy and she didn't want to fall again. She said she would ask Ben's dad to take him at the weekend.

9

The Rowan Tree And The Kingfisher

It rained for the next few days, so Ben stayed indoors. He played his computer games, which was fun, but he missed Jess. The bad weather kept on, so the trip to the stream had to be put off for another week. He was worried that he'd never find the plants in time. Mum had some holidays from work and took him out to the cinema and the museum, and he liked that, but he still wanted to start searching.

On the following Sunday the sun was shining and there were lots of fluffy white clouds in the sky. In the afternoon Gran told Ben to fetch his coat and boots as she wanted him to walk along the lane with her to Mrs Jenkins's house. Ben made a funny face. He liked Mrs Jenkins, but when she started talking with Gran they could be there for hours!

'Come on,' she winked at him, 'it's nice enough weather for you take Scoot into the park to play ball.'

Ben opened his mouth. He'd almost forgotten about the rowan trees in the park. Clever Gran! His hands were shaking as he went to open the door. He remembered his notebook where he'd written how to keep the plants fresh, so he unhooked his rucksack and took that as well. Scoot barked and jumped around them as they went down the garden path. When they reached Mrs Jenkins's house Gran told Ben to go into the park, but nowhere else. She said she could see him from the kitchen window.

Ben and Scoot raced into the park and across to the fence at the far end of the grass. There were three rowan trees on the park side of the fence, and two in the farmer's field. Ben threw the ball for Scoot and then he knelt down under the trees. He moved slowly, pushing the grass apart with his hands, but he couldn't see anything that looked like the Fairy Wing Flowers. Scoot came back with the ball and jumped up at him.

Ben wanted to have a look under the two trees that were in the next field. He wasn't supposed to go out of the park, but he threw Scoot's ball so that it landed right next to the trees and the dog chased after it. Ben followed and started to look for the flowers again. He was hot and there seemed to be lots of flies on this side of the fence.

Just then a small dragonfly landed on his hand. He kept very still and watched its wings shaking. He looked more closely and saw a tiny face scowling at him. A very angry face! It wasn't a dragonfly at all. It was a fairy, and it seemed to be trying to tell him something, but he just couldn't hear it.

Ben looked around. He would have to use the rhyme to become small again. It was the only way that he could ask the fairy for help. He put his hand against the tree trunk and the fairy floated away. He said the rhyme and waited for the dizziness to pass.

'Who are you?' the fairy shouted at him. 'Why are you here and what are you looking for?'

Ben told the fairy all about the Spider Prince and the magic potion. The fairy calmed down, and told him that, many years before, the Spider Wizard had helped the fairies to find a new home after their rowan tree had been hit by lightning. The fairies were very grateful, so she showed Ben where the flowers were. She helped him to collect the seven petals and to wrap them in a dandelion leaf to keep them fresh. Ben thanked her, said the rhyme quickly, and soon he was running back towards Mrs Jenkins's house, with his precious parcel of Fairy Wing petals in his rucksack.

The following Thursday Ben's dad was at home. He told Ben that they could go bird watching if he liked and Scoot could go as well. Gran had told him that Ben wanted to see the kingfishers again, so they set off for the stream in the woods. They walked for quite a long way, so everyone was tired when they reached the place where they'd seen the bird before. Dad sat down to read his newspaper and Scoot lay at his feet. Ben said that he was going to sit nearer the stream, and his dad told him to be careful and not to fall in.

Ben sat very quietly, and after about ten minutes he saw a flash of colour on the other side of the stream. He sat up straight. Yes! There it was again! The kingfisher dived into the stream and came out with a little fish in its beak. It landed on a branch and seemed to be looking straight at Ben. Then it hopped to another branch and put its head on one side.

Ben stood up slowly. He looked around and saw that his dad and Scoot were both sleeping, so he crossed the stream carefully. He stepped from one stone to another until he was on the other side, then he walked along the path until he was underneath the tree where the bird was perched. Ben whistled quietly and the bird looked down at him, then dropped the fish onto the ground. Ben went to pick it up, but when he stretched out his hand he felt a sharp sting.

'Ouch!' he cried. 'That hurt.' He thought there

was a stinging nettle in the grass, but when he looked again he could see lots of insects buzzing around a small silver bush. He stepped back but the insects followed him. He was just about to hit at them with his hand when he remembered what Gran had read about the fern. It was silver and made from the breath of little green dragons. Perhaps these weren't insects at all!

Ben was a little bit afraid to use the rhyme this time. Even though the fairy had been angry with him at first she didn't seem as scary as the dragons. What if they attacked him when he was small? Perhaps they wouldn't listen to him. He looked up at the kingfisher.

'Can you help?' he called to the bird. 'Can you tell them that I need seven leaves of the fern to save the Spider Prince's life?'

The bird dived down into the swarm of dragons. They circled around Ben's head three times, then they disappeared into a hole in the tree trunk. The kingfisher flew to the bush and snapped off a small branch with his beak. He dropped it at Ben's feet and flew away. When Ben picked up the branch he saw that it had exactly seven leaves on it. He took out some more dandelion leaves from his rucksack, and wrapped up the fern. Then he crossed back over the stream and lay down next to Scoot.

He was so excited! He had found two of the ingredients for the magic potion, but he knew that the third one would be the hardest of all to find.

10

Scoot Gives Jess A Fright

On Saturday morning Ben took his rucksack and went to sit under the trees at the bottom of his garden. He only had one more day to collect the seven tears and he really didn't think he could do it. If Jess had come over to play he'd planned to bump into her so that she fell over. He'd hoped that she might cry. He knew that wasn't a very nice thing to do but he wanted to help the spiders so much. He'd asked his gran if she could help, but she didn't think her tears would count.

He felt a tickle on his hand and he jumped. It was Lox. Ben told him that he didn't have all the ingredients just yet, and asked how he could let Lox know if he did find them in time. Lox told Ben to come to the spider gate and flash his torch beam three times. The guards would fetch Lox straight away.

Ben threw the ball a few times for Scoot but he didn't really feel like playing. He sat with his back against the tree and closed his eyes. He felt a soft

53

touch on his cheek. It came again and Ben opened his eyes. It was Jess.

'Jess!' Ben jumped up. 'What are you doing here? I thought Kelly was coming to stay with you for the second week of the holidays?'

Jess smiled at him. 'She was, but we had a terrible argument when I was at her house and my mum brought me home. I wanted to come over before this, but I didn't think you'd want to be friends any more. I wasn't very nice to you, was I?'

'That's all right,' Ben said. 'I'm glad you came. What changed your mind?'

'It was your gran, she rang my mum.'

Ben grinned at her. He said he didn't have time to tell her everything, but he did tell her about the three ingredients and asked her if she thought she could cry!

She tried thinking about sad things but Ben was watching her so closely that all she did was laugh. Then Ben had an idea. He ran up the path to the kitchen and asked his gran to peel an onion for him. He wrapped it in a tissue and went back down the garden.

'Here,' he said, 'this might help. Gran always cries when she peels onions. Let me find the tube that the wizard gave me to catch the tears.' He opened his rucksack. 'Oh no! They won't fit in here.' He held up the tiny tube. 'Why didn't it get bigger when I said the rhyme? Everything else in my bag did. It must be a magic tube.'

'What can we do?' Jess asked. 'If it has to be seven tears, we need a bigger tube.'

Ben scratched his head, then he looked at Jess and grinned. He knew exactly what to do, but would Jess agree?

'Hold the tube, Jess,' he told her. 'What if I make you smaller so that your tears will be tiny and then the tube will be big enough?'

Jess looked puzzled. 'What do mean? How can you make me small?'

'I'll tell you all about it later,' Ben promised. 'Gran gave me the secret and now I can make myself, or anyone else, smaller and then bigger. It doesn't hurt and it won't take long. You just need to smell the onion and then catch seven tears in the tube. As soon as you've done it, I'll make you big again.'

Jess looked worried but she said she'd do it. Ben put the onion next to her feet and made sure that she had the tube in her hands. He said the magic rhyme quietly and did the actions. Jess watched him with her eyes wide open. Then she felt a tingling in her arms and legs and she felt dizzy, so she sat down quickly and closed her eyes. When she opened them she could see two very large shoes next to her. She looked up. Ben was a giant!

Jess was very scared but she remembered what she had to do. She leaned against the onion and took a deep breath. She poked out her tongue. Yuk! She breathed in again and could feel her eyes starting to water, but there were still no tears. She tried twice more and finally the tears began to roll down her cheeks. She took the stopper from the tube and carefully caught seven tears. Then she put the stopper back.

Ben knelt down on the ground and took the tube from Jess. He put it in his rucksack and he was just about to say the rhyme to bring Jess back, when Scoot dashed across the grass and picked her up by the hood of her coat. He shook her a few times and Ben could hear her screaming.

'Drop that Scoot,' he shouted. 'Naughty dog! Give it to me now.'

Scoot put his head on one side and looked at Ben. He didn't understand. This was a new toy, wasn't it? He ran around the tree three times, but when he saw that Ben wasn't playing their usual game of chase, he stopped. He walked towards Ben with his tail down, and then he dropped Jess on the ground.

Ben said the rhyme as quickly as he could and waited for Jess to feel steady on her feet. She was really crying now.

'I'm so sorry Jess,' he said. 'I didn't see Scoot behind the tree. Are you all right?'

Jess sniffed and wiped her eyes on her sleeve. 'I'm all covered in dog spit so, no, I am not all right.'

Ben couldn't help laughing. Her hair was all spiky and she looked like she'd been out in the rain. Jess pretended to be angry but after a while she started laughing as well.

'I don't know why I'm friends with you,' she said. 'You always get me into trouble, but we do have some fun, don't we?'

Ben told her that he had to call for Lox to come out, and said that she should sit down next to the tree. He didn't know if Lox would come right out if she was there but they'd have to try. He lay down on the ground and wriggled under the hedge. He shone the torch beam on the spider gate at the back of the hedge and blinked it on and off three times. Then he wriggled out again and went to sit next to Jess. Five minutes later Lox peeped out from the hedge.

'It's all right Lox,' Ben whispered. 'This is Jess. She's the one who helped me last year with finding the last piece of the spider gate, and she's just helped me now. I couldn't have done it on my own. Please don't be afraid of her.'

Lox came towards them slowly and told Ben that it was all right for Jess to be there. He thanked her for helping Ben. Jess held her breath. She felt as though she was in a dream. It was so strange to hear this spider talking to them. She shook her head and just watched as Lox took the three ingredients. He told Ben and Jess to wait in the garden and ten minutes later he was back. He ran towards them waving his front legs in the air.

'You did it,' he told Ben. 'You really did it. The wizard was so excited that he ran up the walls of the cave and spun a golden-coloured web all over the ceiling. Queen Aranya was crying and everyone else was cheering for you. The only one who wasn't happy with you was Spindra, but we're watching her very carefully.'

'Who's Spindra?' Jess asked, but Ben said he'd tell her later. She rolled her eyes.

Lox carried on talking. 'The queen would like to thank you both but we don't think it's safe for you to come into the kingdom again. She asked if you could be in the garden after dark tonight? If you can, be here when the owl starts to hoot. We'll be waiting and you won't have to stay out for long. There are some others who'd like to meet you as well.'

Lox ran back under the hedge. Jess pulled at Ben's sleeve.

'Oh boy,' she said. 'You have so much to tell me. I want to know everything NOW!'

Ben laughed. 'All right bossy, but we'd better go back indoors. I think you need to wash your face before anyone sees you. Then we have to think of a way to meet Lox and the others.'

11

The Barbecue And The Owl

Later that day Ben and Jess were lying on the floor in the living room. They were looking at the book from the library and Ben was telling Jess about the things that had happened to him. He remembered what his gran had said about the secret so he didn't tell her everything, just most of it. Gran had telephoned Jess's mum and they'd agreed that Jess could stay the night at Ben's house.

'What are you going to do?' Jess asked him. 'How are we going to be able to go out when it's dark?'

Ben sat up. 'Well, we could ask if Dad would do a barbecue for us, like he did for my birthday last year. It's still a bit cold but it's not raining. I could put up my tent near the tree and we could play at being explorers like before, but we wouldn't have to go outside the garden this time.'

Jess nodded. 'What time does it get dark? What if the owl doesn't start hooting until really late?'

Ben went into the kitchen and asked his gran

when it would be dark. She told him it would be about half past six. Then he went to find his dad who was cleaning the car. Dad said that they could have a barbecue as a special treat, as it was almost the last day of the holidays, and they could stay up a bit later as well. He and Ben found the camping light and then the tent and they called to Jess to help them put it up.

At six o'clock Ben's dad lit the barbecue and Mum and Gran brought out the food. Scoot had been shut in the house because he could be very naughty when the family ate outside, and always tried to steal the sausages. Ben and Jess helped with the plates, but they were so excited that they kept giggling together. The grown-ups thought it was because of the barbecue. Well, it was a bit, but Ben and Jess were thinking about who might be waiting under the hedge.

When the food was cooked, Mum put two plates onto a tray and two glasses of fruit juice. Gran put on some bread rolls, some sausages and chicken, and then two muffins. Dad carried the tray to the tent and Ben and Jess scrambled inside.

'There you are,' Dad said. 'Eat it while it's hot. We're going to eat in the kitchen. You can stay out for an hour, but come in sooner if you're too cold.'

Ben and Jess ate their food and drank some juice. They were just going to start on their muffins when Jess pulled on Ben's sleeve. She put her finger in front of her lips.

'Shhhh. Listen,' she said. 'It's the owl. I can hear the owl!'

Ben listened. It sounded as though the owl was right above them. They crept out of the tent and looked up. There he was, on a branch near the top of the tree. He turned his head and looked right at them with his big round eyes. Ben had never seen an owl as close as this before and he wanted to look at it for longer, but there was something swinging in front of his face.

Ben jumped back. It was Lox. The spider landed on Ben's shoulder and began to talk into his ear.

'Everyone's waiting for you,' he said, 'but they're a little bit afraid to come out.'

'Afraid? Why are they afraid of me? I helped them, didn't I?'

Lox said it was because Ben was now so much bigger than the spiders, but he did have an idea.

'If you could use the magic again, then everyone would be happy. They'd like to meet Jess as well.'

'What about Spindra?' Ben asked. 'I don't want to be small when I meet her again.'

Lox told Ben that the queen's sister had been sent away, so she wouldn't be able to hurt them. Ben sat down on the ground. He knew he could only use the rhymes seven times in his whole life, so he counted on his fingers.

'Once when I went into the kingdom, once with the rowan tree fairy, and once to catch Jess's tears.'

If he did what Lox had asked he would have to use the magic twice more – once for him and once for Jess. That would be five times. He'd be like Gran, using up nearly all his chances in the first year, but he really wanted to meet Queen Aranya. He wondered if he could go on his own but then he felt mean. Jess was his best friend again, and if she hadn't helped him he wouldn't be here now.

He told Lox that he'd do it, and asked Jess if she wanted to come. She looked scared but said she would. Ben said the rhyme for Jess, then for himself. They laughed at each other when they were small. Jess said that Ben looked like someone in the story about the people who lived under the floorboards of a big house.

Lox told Ben and Jess to stay in front of the tent. He ran under the hedge and a few moments later he ran out again.

'Come on.' He waved to them. 'They're waiting at the entrance.'

12

Ben And Jess Receive A Present

Ben and Jess followed Lox under the hedge. When they reached the spider gate it was wide open and Lox waved them in. They could hardly believe their eyes. There were glow worms all around the walls so it was easy to see what was happening. In the middle of the big entrance room was Queen Aranya. The wizard was next to her. Above their heads was a silver cobweb, and bouncing around in it was a tiny spider. It was the Spider Prince!

Lox called Ben and Jess over to his side. 'You can meet the visitors first, and then the queen will speak to you.'

He turned around and Jess gasped. In front of her was the most beautiful fairy. She had golden hair, golden wings, a green and gold dress, and bright green shoes. Lox said that she was Tianna Rowan, the Fairy Queen of the Rowan clan. Next to her was another fairy who looked almost the same, but she had silver wings, a red dress, and red shoes. She was Shaylee Rowan, the Fairy Princess.

The fairies touched fingers with Ben and Jess and fluttered their wings.

Lox moved on to the next group and Ben's heart began to thump when he saw who it was. Two green dragons stood side by side and were staring at him. When he'd seen them before they'd been small, but they had still managed to bite him. Now he was small and they looked enormous. He stood behind Lox, who said that they were Lulong Zeewang, the Green Dragon King, and Lulong Tyzee, the Dragon Prince. The dragons nodded their heads. As Ben passed them he could feel the back of his neck tingling from their cold breath. He noticed that Jess didn't stand near them for long either.

Then the wizard made a speech about how brave Ben had been, and Queen Aranya moved forward. She thanked Ben and Jess for helping to make the prince better and said that she had a gift for them. The wizard handed her a golden-coloured cobweb. It was the one that he had spun when Lox had brought him the three ingredients. The queen broke it and gave half to Ben and half to Jess. She told them to hold it out in front of them.

The wizard ran around in a circle three times then he held up his two front legs and waved them over the pieces of web. He said some words that Ben didn't understand and the web began to glow. Jess was shaking as the web grew heavier and heavier. When the wizard stopped moving, Lox helped Ben and Jess to carry the pieces to the spider gate. They turned around and saw that everyone was waving to them, so they waved too.

Back at the tent, Lox told them to take care of their gifts. The wizard's magic had turned the cobweb into gold. It would only be small in the human world, but it was still something precious. He told Ben that he would come to the window sill the next night, when it would be the full moon. He thanked Jess again, then he ran back under the hedge and out of sight.

Ben and Jess were very tired, so Ben said the growing bigger rhyme very quickly for both of them. They went back into the tent to look at their gifts.

'It's a bit like the spider gate piece,' Jess said. 'The one we found in the woods.'

Ben agreed. 'Yes, but I don't think that was gold. What will you do with yours?'

'I don't know yet,' she said. 'I think I'll put it somewhere safe until I'm older.'

'Me too,' said Ben. 'Come on, we'd better go back to the house.'

The next night Ben was in his bedroom at eight o'clock. Mum had said that he could look at his book for ten minutes, but instead he pulled back the curtain and looked for Lox. The spider was waiting in the corner, so Ben opened the window quietly.

'Look up, Ben,' Lox told him.

There, high in the sky, hung the moon. It looked like a big golden balloon floating over the tops of the trees.

'Every time you see the moon like that,' Lox said, 'you'll know that everyone in the spider kingdom is thinking of you – especially me. We hope you won't forget us, and perhaps one day we can meet again. Goodbye, Ben. Goodbye.'

Lox ran out of the window, over the ledge, and was gone.

Ben didn't have time to say anything, so he just whispered, 'Goodbye.'

He looked up at the moon again, and just for a moment he was sure it was covered with a golden cobweb.

Ben's Shrinking Rhyme

Hold my breath and count to four,
breathe out slow and count four more.
Turn three circles, count to ten,
touch the floor, turn once again.
Close my eyes and touch my nose,
now make me small from head to toes!

Read on to see what Ben and Jess do next

Ben and the Spider Lake

In the summer holidays Ben, his family, his dog Scoot, and his best friend Jess, stay in a cottage near the Dark Mountains. Ben and Jess find out that there's a lake inside the mountain called Spider Lake and they wonder if it's the place that Ben's Gran had told him about in the spring, when she gave him the power to make himself small so that he could help the Spider Wizard to save the Spider Prince. Scoot gets into trouble when he finds a way through a cave onto the path around the lake where Ben and Jess meet a white owl called Hiboo and a mysterious lady.

When Ben arrives home he finds out that the lane at the back of his garden is going to be dug up. He's worried because he knows that the spiders who live under the lane will lose their home and could even be hurt. He has to find Lox, the guardian of the spider kingdom to tell him what's going to happen. Ben and Jess try desperately to think of somewhere that the spiders could live but they only have four weeks before the workmen arrive. Can they find a safe home for the spiders in time? If they do, how will they move them? Is there anyone who could help? Maybe Gran has some ideas.

Ben walked into the cave very carefully. The floor was bumpy and there were pools of water everywhere. He shone his torch beam along the walls and he could see that there were lots of little passageways in the rock. He listened again and could hear Scoot barking.

Ben squeezed through the tunnel. When he stood up he couldn't believe what he saw. Lots and lots of water. He knew right away that this was the lake. This was really Spider Lake! Scoot was standing on a big stone. He was barking at something in the grass. Ben ran towards him and caught hold of his collar. Lying in the grass was a white bird. Ben knew it was an owl.

'Oh Scoot. What have you done?'

Find out more in September 2016

Did you miss Ben's first adventure?
Turn over to learn how he met Lox for the first time.

Ben and the Spider Gate

Ben loves chatting to his wise gran, playing computer games with his best friend Jess, and helping his dad to train his clever dog Scoot. Best of all though, he likes playing ball in the garden with Scoot.

Then one hot, summer day Ben meets Lox, the gate-keeper of the spider kingdom under the garden hedge. Lox desperately needs Ben's help before the end of the autumn, but can Ben save the spider kingdom without leaving the garden and going into the deep, dark wood? The leaves are starting to fall, and Ben and Jess must take a brave decision if the spiders are to have a safe winter.

Talking to Gran, Ben begins to suspect that she might know more about his quest than she's admitting.

Ben threw the ball high in the air and Scoot jumped up after it and then chased it down the garden path. The sun was hot and after a while Scoot lay down in the shade of the garden shed and rested his head on his paws. Ben began to feel sleepy as well and his eyes started to close.

When he opened them again he thought he was still asleep and dreaming. He wasn't a big boy any more, he was a very little boy. He wasn't much bigger than one of the daisies that were growing in the grass!